A Poetry Collection

WORLD'S A
MURDERER

SIMRAN DEV

BLUEROSE PUBLISHERS
India | U.K.

Copyright © Simran Dev 2025

All rights reserved by author. No part of this publication may be reproduced, stored in a retrieval system or transmitted in any form or by any means, electronic, mechanical, photocopying, recording or otherwise, without the prior permission of the author. Although every precaution has been taken to verify the accuracy of the information contained herein, the publisher assumes no responsibility for any errors or omissions. No liability is assumed for damages that may result from the use of information contained within.

BlueRose Publishers takes no responsibility for any damages, losses, or liabilities that may arise from the use or misuse of the information, products, or services provided in this publication.

For permissions requests or inquiries regarding this publication, please contact:

BLUEROSE PUBLISHERS
www.BlueRoseONE.com
info@bluerosepublishers.com
+91 8882 898 898
+4407342408967

ISBN: 978-93-6783-147-2

Cover design: Yash Singhal
Typesetting: Namrata Saini

First Edition: February 2025

Preface

As I delve into the world of words, I've come to realize that poetry is the delicate dance between self-awareness and vulnerability. It's the brave act of embracing our deepest emotions, allowing them to blossom or decay, leaving an indelible mark on our souls.

This collection is a reflection of my own journey, a candid exploration of mistakes, nostalgia, love, and loss. Within these pages, I invite you to immerse yourself in the ebb and flow of my inner world.

May these words resonate with you, and may you discover the beauty and vulnerability that lies within.

—Simran Dev

Trigger Warning!!

Some poems deal with mature themes, emotional distress, and graphic imagery. Before reading, remember your mental health matters.

(But let's be real, you're probably going to ignore this warning and dive headfirst into the emotional abyss anyway).

Contents

Sparks Within 1

   The Weeping Sky 2

   Ghosts of Yesterday 4

   What Remained 5

   The World has killed, but 6

   A Silent Treatment 7

   Love From a Beach 9

   An Angel's Plea 11

   Merchandise 12

   Beauty? 14

   We Won't Fall 16

Unveiled 17

   The Weight of Quiet 18

   Unknown 19

   Bonfire Smoke 20

   Us that we once were 21

   Clouds of Regret 22

   If I could write the rest of my life... 23

   Do You Feel Me? 25

   A Ride 27

   Take me back 28

   A Call 30

Phlegmatic Ache 33
The Language of Tears 34
Fading Gleams 36
The Silence Between Us 37
A hand? 38
No I don't 39
Splendid Childhood 40
I hope you know 42
Not Mine 43
Non Existent 44
Risen without a Breath 45

The Sane Blood Bath 47
Her Lullaby 48
A Grey Game 49
Band Aid 51
The Right Way 52
(Pain)ter 53
Battle 54
Escaping Boys 55
If My Heart Were a Person 56
Devoted to Nothing 57
The World is a Murderer 58

Sparks Within

The Weeping Sky

It's the time of the year,
The lazy July,
Where heart breaks and bonds,
Some cry and fly.

Generations have passed,
And how beautifully we've grown
Technologies and machines are everywhere,
But Gods are unknown.

Cultures are lost,
Traditions have died;
Filths are not only on earth,
But also in every other mind.

Murders and rivalries,
Rapes and deaths,
Toxicity and abuse,
Love has become threats.

I know I'm not perfect
But at least I don't harm,
If I call for world peace,
It will be nothing but a false alarm,

Hereby I write,
About everything that's going wrong,
But here's an advice-
Never stop being kind,
Never stop being strong.

Remember God loves us,
And karma is true
Ask for anything with a pure heart,
He'll give it to you.

He made sun for light,
And moon for nights;
Stars that gleam ,
Rivers and streams.

He lets himself cut
For our roofs,
Don't talk to me again
If you ask for proofs.

Now when I look around,
I'm left with no words to speak,
I felt bad and I cried,
And he made the darn sky weep.

Ghosts of Yesterday

Here beneath the moonlit sky I lay,
Listening the songs we used to play;
Hovering my hand over the grasses, I cry,
Feeling your absence, remembering the promises we made.

They haunt every corner of my mind,
Reminders of love, both gentle and unkind;
Memories flicker like swaying flames,
As if Ghosts of yesterday are calling our names.

Reaching out to tell us how stupid we were
To become cold and still burn;
I'm sorry, can we please extinguish that flame?
They are calling us darling, the Ghosts of Yesterday;

I'll keep my promise to forever be with you,
Please don't break yours, please don't make me someone you knew.

What Remained

In forgotten corners
Our shadows hide
From the world
Which only subsides;

Surely we'll leave hands through the fight
And hold them again after we've survived.

The apocalypse won't be easy
Heck of a tough battle;
But think how we'd rest in the breeze,
Head on shoulders,
After everything has been tackled.

And when the world finally ends,
Engulfed in flood or flames,
Extinguished to nothingness
Or freezes in the hurricane;

Then I'll look at you,
More grateful than ever to have you as my friend.

And when we're totally dead and decayed,
The earth will bear flowers like popping champagne,
And hell, our souls will devour their pollen,
For we must've died, but they will forever remain.

The World has killed, but

I know that life exists
And I love to describe it in verses,
Surely, the world has upsetted everyone
But think about why only we were pushed out of our mother's cervix?

See life's a present to everyone
What matters is how you perceive it
With excitement or care,
Or disappointment or despair;

Don't want to woe your younger self anymore?
So what you thought to become once,
Now is the time to be it.

See the world has killed
And it will kill
But without this bastard murderer,
We wouldn't exist.

A Silent Treatment

"Why? Please!
Just listen for once!"
Fighting the urge
To say these words;

Formed perfectly on my lips
But Scared to be revealed
I've been this way for ages—
Completely sealed.

Of course I won't utter,
Not even a single sigh
I'm fully silenced
With hopes you can read eyes.
But you can't, well, not anymore
So I let you go.

Yes it does ache
But loving doesn't mean you have to break.
And boy I'm far more than just broken,
Always a choice, never even chosen.

I'm bleeding and you're blind
I'm drowning and you're flying
I never showed you the ocean
You didn't show me your sky

I'll hold my sorrow, so you don't have to share,
Because I don't want you to fight the tears
You don't wish to shed.

Love From a Beach

Sometimes I wonder—
What is it like to be sand?
Well don't call me crazy
I like to be away from human land.

Imagine this—
You're not even earth
And nor even ocean,
Sometimes a castle's birth
Sometimes carried like a potion.

Swallowing tears
And prints of lovers ,
Cigarettes and alcohol ,
Joys and suffers;

Probably hiding troves
Filled with sweat and treasures,
All for the love
That's beyond the measure.

You gleam golden under the sun
And blue under the moon;
Loved by almost everyone
And some others will soon too

If I'd ever want to be something on earth,
Sand is what I'll be,
I want to be loved without conditions,
I want love carefree.

An Angel's Plea

Congratulations,
You know how to love,
Yet you're puzzled
Don't really know what for;

You just keep on giving
And it never stops,
Sweetheart you need to stop running
Before you get lost.

You feel there's no way out
And you care too much,
Can't even cry or shout
So you sit there just hurt.
I can't change your actions,
Perhaps your mind is where I can aim;
Please love yourself,
And stop with self-blames.

Till when will you point your bads out?
Till when will you drain?
Please try to flourish,
Before you decay.

Merchandise

My son asked-
"How much did it cost, to get this?"
I replied-
"Just a lifetime, that's it."

Took a heartbreak to believe,
A betrayal to leave,
A speed to cease,
A decrease to increase.

Loved and lost,
Lost and loved again,
Coin of challenges I tossed
And realised I was the answer to all my quests.

After a million tries,
I climbed that wall,
The one that I kept falling from.

The things I've faced,
Were water to my growth,
Pain I embraced,
Kindly murdering the wroth.

So it did cost me a lot;
Sold tears for strength,
Sold wars for saught,
Sold the broken for a mend.

Now what I want you to do-
Is to sell love where you feel safe;
Because we all are some sort of merchants
And we often make wrong trades.

Beauty?

Is everything beauty?
Like perfect eyes & perfect lips,
Perfect smile & perfect body?

The way you talk?
Or the confidence written by our walks?
Who do we represent?
Ever gave a second thought?

An Angel's heart,
A devil's mind,
Painting an almost unreal art—
What do you want?!

You determine a soul
By the skin that it has worn?
Embarrassing that you don't know,
That we're just spirits in different fonts;

In the dress we love,
With the drinks we like,
It can be coffee,
Or either wine;

Let them wear makeup,
You fix your tie,
And off you go,
While loving your life.

What is this judgment?
It makes no sense—
Guess if you'd try to open your heart,
Probably then it wouldn't be this dense;

Because you call people crazy
Who love a soul not their body
It's like calling me crazy,
For savouring wine instead of bitter coffee.

We Won't Fall

You know I'm scared too,
I'm haunted by my thoughts,
But screw everything,
Let's give it a shot.

Where oceans are bluer,
And skies are brighter,
Why wouldn't I chase flames
Instead of barely burning fires?

Let's walk towards life,
There are some lessons left to learn,
Where I was struggling to breathe,
Gracefully the breaths you've returned.

I'm thrilled to the core,
I'm chilled by the cold,
But heck I'll skate,
If your hands are what I'll hold

Glide smoothly with me,
Let's risk it all,
If it works it works,
If we fall we fall.

Unveiled

The Weight of Quiet

How much silence do I hold?
How many stories are there, untold?
It's so light to call me fragile,
Feels heavy when I ask- who are you, except alive?

You call the man foolish for glaring into the sun,
Yes he wants to be blinded, yes he wants to be burned;

Go on and laugh and call him crazy,
Only he knows the courage it took to escape his misery.

How many nights passed by,
How many times he winced;
How many times he bowed down
How many times he sinned.

All in a silence Along with puzzled wrong and rights,
Life crushed him
With the weights of the quiet.

Unknown

Am I abnormal? To live in a house and search for a home?
I feel so little watching myself trapped between the grown,
And everywhere I look, I have no place to go,
So who am I? Where do I belong?

I'm like the leaves you must've stepped on,
I'm like the footprints you left behind,
I'm like the fist you made when you were angry,
I just simply exist from time to time.

You can find my shoulder anywhere, but you'll never see me relying on one,
You may find me with animals and birds, when it comes to trusting humans, I'd say none.

For some you might seem way too fragile,
For some you might be way too strong,
Then you're left with this knot in your head
Which seems like it cannot be solved.

Sometimes I talk too much, sometimes not at all,
Sometimes I'd take the leap, sometimes I'm scared of the fall;
Unravel me and you shall find the tangles not shown,
And to me I'd stay forever unknown.

Bonfire Smoke

I remember the December camp,
All the dancing, singing, the food and drinks,
I was miles away,
But still you were the only thing I could think.

You flashed before my eyes
As the booze kicked in,
All the laughter faded,

The lighter flicked
Burned into flames ,
And the fire was born;

And there I went— running back to everything I was trying to escape from.

Us that we once were

Our fire that once embarrassed the sun
Now has no potential to even warm anyone,
Our light that sparkled brighter than the stars
Faded away like declining beats of hearts.

Did we die?
Or just escaped life?
God knows
And we're left wondering why.

Clouds of Regret

Blackened lips
Cigarette still hanging loose,
I know that they don't care
But to accept it, I refuse.

It's better to be lonely with someone
Than to be left completely abandoned
Don't know if my parents are proud,
Actually, I know they're totally baffled.

They won't be back until we apologize,
Oh how I sabotage myself in my own paradise.

Ensnared in the cage I built,
But hey it's not so bad,
Just clouds of regrets and the rains of guilt.

If I could write the rest of my life…

If I could write the rest of my life
I'd add little flowers
To make it colourful enough,
I'd add more animals
Who didn't get any love

If I could write the rest of my life
I'd spend more time beneath the shades,
Feel more protected by nature
Pushing people away.

If I could write the rest of my life
I'd surely pick up that pen without concern
Of what might happen next,
I'd do whatever I feel is undone.

I'd write beneath the gleaming sun,
I won't care about the burn,
If I love light how can I not bare?
And then I won't be afraid of your stares.

Your eyes, your words,
Oh you speak so loud,
And that's not your reason, you're just way too proud,

And I hope, I'd never have to fake smiles anymore,
And I hope, I'd never have to yell till my throat gets sore,
Embarrassing myself explaining how I don't feel their care,
Perhaps if I could write the rest of my life,
I simply won't be there.

Do You Feel Me?

When a notification lights up your phone
But it's not me, asking you about your day?
Do you feel me?
When her hair is now with what you play?

Do you smell her fragrance?
Is it similar to mine?
And you realize it isn't me
As soon as you open your eyes?

Do you feel me?
When she holds your arm?
Tracing her fingers around on your body?
Do you shield her the way you did to me?

Do you feel me?
When you listen to the artist
We both once loved?
Do you feel me?
Whenever she giggles at your words?

Do you feel me?
When she rests her head on your shoulder?
And you say 'it'll all be fine'
Do you feel me?
When you kiss her
And her lips are not mine?

A Ride

Let's go on a ride,
And never come back,
Let the world divide,
While we travel our track.

Take a seat on my veins,
And travel to my heart,
It's filled with our moments
Where our love is collaged.

You'll be blown away with the light,
That you've bloomed me with,
I'm Icarus to your sun,
And this one's not a myth.

Now let's go through my mind,
Just ignore the mess,
I'll show you what happened to it,
When we first met.

You see those colours?
You see those blasts?
Yeah, they still shine with the thought of you,
Even when we didn't last.

Take me back

Something sweet happened,
I saw him again,
Admiring the same painting,
Until our glances exchanged;

Same eyes brown honey,
Same scent still alluring,
Rigged out in all black,
Had me reminiscing.

The beaches and mountains,
And that café with chimes;
Late night dinner,
With ravioli and wine;
The spring, the winters,
Those snowy sunset skies;
Singing and swaying,
With your hand in mine.

Our soul's oneness
Was beyond strong,
Now we're just strangers,
With hearts that don't belong.

Once thought of our daughter's eyes,
Who's would she wear;
Definitely not mine now,
They've become a distant stare.

I turned back to the painting,
Letting out the memories with a sigh;
How can you know someone so much,
And not at all at the same time?

A Call

Pigeon oh pigeon!
Take away these letters,
These letters I write,
Fly up and then scatter;

Scatter them in the air,
All over the world,
Perhaps who'll catch,
Will know they're heard.

I hear their call,
And I write them all,
But don't tell them
It was me who spalled;

Spalled their heart—
That fake rock heart,
Into a beating one
So they can restart.

Pigeon oh pigeon!
Do this after my death,
Call them after
I've taken my last breath;

All my life
I've been the one and only,
Let the readers come,
Let me be a bit less lonely.

Phlegmatic Ache

The Language of Tears

Bleeding literature from our eyes,
Oh, who'd read it except our mirrors?
What we look at when we peel of our disguise
And see the lungs filled with smoke and kidneys filled with liquor.

I hate how foreign I become
When it comes to the language of hurt;
My words stumble against the pain of translation
And I'm left with silence louder than my explanation.

Everyday I switch personalities
Like the dresses I wear,
Which words go here,
What accent goes there,
Some days a bookworm, others a music freak,
I try to do my best to be whatever,
Except to be me.

I'm a chaos myself, I'll go hide and you go seek,
Whatever you do, you'll never find me.
Yes I'll surely give you a call,

A voice of glances, and you won't get it at all.
Myself, I'll come in your way for you to see,
You'll never understand the language that my eyes speak.

Fading Gleams

Our love was a bridge of ebb and flow,
But why is it this time that you let it go?
Can you easily cinder everything to ashes?
And leave our list blank, with just dashes?

Well it's okay, I won't fight anymore,
I've had enough wars where you didn't even show;

So I'm departing now,
Separating our combine,
A memory of warmth
That once did shine.

The Silence Between Us

I said that you looked good in red
And you wore it the next day,
I complimented you again
And you blushed in a certain way.

Oh you shared a lot; your jacket, pens and cookies,
And you looked at me with eyes that said –'Oh what a wonder we could be'

So why don't you say it?
Why don't you say
That you prefer hoodies over jackets?
That you prefer to write on your tab?
Why do you bring the cookies of the flavour you hate?
When your whole closet is blue, why do you even wear red?
You should say what you wish to convey,

But maybe in silence is where you find your solace.
You'll be left with words you could've said,
And I'll remember you, whenever I see something red.

What tomorrow brings, who knows,
You'll never speak
And I'll let this silence grow.

A hand?

Why do you crave roses when you fear to grasp the thorns?
You said those words anyway when you clearly knew they'd haunt,
Haunt that piece of my mind
For which to search I'd give my whole life
But I'm tangled myself, so tell me why?
Tell me why do you dream to touch skies
When you can't even take a flight?

I knew you were scared,
Scared to flee
And you knew I'd help,
But you never wanted it from me.

No I don't

No I don't love you,
I didn't abandon my friends to watch you play
No I don't love you,
I just wanted to watch the game.

No I don't love you,
I just checked the weather before going out
And kept an umbrella just in case.

No I don't love you,
You just bumped into me when it rained,
No I don't love you,
Out of kindness I asked if you're okay.

No I don't love you,
I was just carrying a towel spare,
You are just a good friend,
That's why I shared.

No I don't love you
I just simply held you by the fire place because you were hurt and cold,

'No I don't love you'
The biggest lie I've ever told.

Splendid Childhood

Lost at the sight of the night sky
When my eyes captured a plane;
I looked up at it as a wide grin spread across my face
"It's crazy how some habits never change"

I thought to myself as I glanced back to these buildings,
Flickered the lighter and I knew,
I wasn't the kid I used to be.
I don't cry anymore like a stupid fool
For some stupid soul to notice
I just let my heart bleed in hypnosis.

Nobody understands so stitch your mouth
Doesn't matter how much this heart has to say,
I inhaled the smoke as it flew along the wind,
"Why did I turn out to be this way?"

Rested my head on the window edge
Looked up to see a spider build a web
Smiled because I wasn't scared of it anymore
Frowned because this house was getting old.

Glanced down at the empty swing
Missed my best friend a bit

Yeah, got a few more years with them
Then probably a happy life I'll live.

Won't need to cover my ears
Or blast music till they hurt,
Or scroll for distraction
Or damage my lungs.

I'll be away from what I fear,
Their presence, that noise,
Or some words like-
"DON'T YOU DARE RAISE YOUR VOICE"

I wouldn't have to control my tears to ruin moods
I wouldn't have to beg to be understood
Exhaled the smoke and realized
"What a splendid fucking childhood"

I hope you know

I miss us,
I miss you everyday;
Although I'm happy now,
But I'd be happier if you stayed.

But hey you're a good friend!
Don't drown in the pool of guilt;
Everything happens for a reason
And soon you'll forget all of it.

Not Mine

"I hate him"
Is what I say to them,
While all I think about
Is our little 'when'

Our little when,
Was a dream come true,
But alas;
Now you're just somebody I knew.

And I hope you know,
That I'll wait,
Loved you too deeply, but what an evil fate.
Maniac I am, in your love,
I can be there for all your daunts,
I can fight everyone that wants you,
But not the one you want.

Non Existent

It's over, we're over,
But I want to relive every moment
We were closer.

Your laughs still echoes,
Without you I deny to get older;
Wish we would've stayed friends,
We destroyed it as lovers.

You were my faith and belief,
And I was the bird you freed;
Alas I fell in love with your façade
And facades don't exist, and so don't we.

Well there's the dead end
But before you go—
Hold my hand, be my friend,

Give me a company,
Or at least let me lend;
But don't suffocate me with the hope—
That we will exist again.

Risen without a Breath

My body was still,
My blood was turning colder,
I slept with such a blitheness,
With no weights upon my shoulder.

It was finally present—
The longing I craved,
And if you were here,
You were never too late.

I've risen and I'm watching,
I hear calls for my name,
Their cries shatter the air,
Am I one to blame?

Death intensified your love for me,
While all my life I travelled a solo track,
No please don't hold my hand now,
This time I can't hold you back.

The Sane Blood Bath

Her Lullaby

Take me back to the days
When life wasn't a maze,
When I lived unafraid
When I left instead of trying to escape.

This invisible choke
Of being the understanding & never the understood,
Will take all of my breaths away
Like hanging without a stool;

But whenever I try,
I remember her tune
The soft humming sound,
And Oh the way it soothed.

Well I guess I'll be choking till I remember,
I hate how I can't forget,
I'll be breathless forever.

Take me in your arms again,
And sing the same song
Until God lifts my soul up

And from there I wave you a goodbye,
I remember your voice so well
I'll make the heavens rain by your Lullaby.

A Grey Game

"Another game?" I asked with my shaky hands
You crunched your nose and said I was very bad,
I smiled and I said 'it's okay' to myself
And you proceeded to wish you had more friends.

Father was your company when you were young,
Stop the sugar-coating, the damage is done.
The genes separated, both are writers, but one's good at sports,
She's got the rage and other couldn't bare anymore.

I apologize because it doesn't make me small
You acted like nothing happened, stood tall,
Got mad and rained hell from your mouth
And for the first time I awaited for your fall
While my eyes couldn't stop shedding salt.

"A weak egoist, very fragile"
Please, I'm barely alive.
You'd rather come up with a million reasons
Than to actually apologize.

But please don't now, too late my dear,
You created something that didn't exist
Now it's your mouth that I fear.

Don't ask me for a game again,
This egoist won't play,

You want me to ignore all the dark,
And light is where I should concentrate
But how am I supposed to do that?
When you've painted the whole sky grey?

Band Aid

Let your inner child scream
Who thought they were everything they shouldn't be
Who fell from the peaks and turned into streams,
Just became whatever their elders wanted them to be.

A slave, a master,
A kid, a parent,
Don't say you love them,
Your fake glass love, nothing but transparent.

Invisible and empty,
You've left them in despair,
Sobbing till they ran out of breath
Don't fix it now,
Stop bandaging the dead.

The Right Way

Such naiveness in her eyes
But she feeds on human brains,
The smell of blood soothes her
And she doesn't want to walk away.

She loves to peel off skins
Until she finds out what's underneath,
Truth oozes it's way out
And she gulps every drop of it.

Knowing it was harmful,
Knowing it was poison,
It would only make her sick and strong,
Feathers in a cage is still a prison.

She bit her parts off saying-
"I deserve to see the day
Where you'd know how I'd bleed
If you held me the right way"

(Pain)ter

I'm a painter
But I hate how I paint a lot
I brush from blades
Into tears and blood loss;

I hate how skilled I am
I can paint in the dark
Sometimes on my bathroom floor
Leaving unseen marks.

Under my shorts
Because wrists are 'attention seeking'
I hate how overjoyed I get
When I get treated like a normal being.

I hope I get over this art
And find another hobby
I wish someone would wish to hark
Guess that will stop the painting on my body.

Battle

Look mom, I'm a soldier,
I'm at a war with myself,
Don't know when will it get over.

Well I hope soon,
Because I can't stop shedding,
The tears you caused me,
It doesn't stop spreading.

You know I'm miserable,
Oh, you probably don't;
For you you've given me
Shelter, roof and clothes.

Maybe I'm only selfish
That's enough what you've given me,
I knew you wouldn't understand
So I kept my battle unseen.

You've lost your daughter
She tried her best,
She was tired alive,
Don't stress her while she rests.

Escaping Boys

Too young to be someone's last,
Too old to be someone's first
And I hate to be the between
Quenching everyone's thirst.

Who'll be there for me?
When I'm loosing all my memories?
I've pictured everything alone,
It feels like an incurable disease.

Every hand I grasp
Always waves goodbyes in the end;
Affections are so alien to me
Even a simple smile stays pend.

I really don't want you to drown in me,
Because I can't help with my own frost,
You'll soon be dead on your feet
In hopes our paths will never be again crossed.

If My Heart Were a Person

If my heart were a person,
It'd be swimming in wealth,
Doling out dollars,
Handing out cash;

Not the ones that are paper made,
But the ones egressed from heart,
Love is to feel, not to display,
It'll teach us this art.

But soon it will tire,
Its wealth spent and worn,
From giving and giving, with no time to mourn;

The weight of each moment,
The difficulty of each test,
Will leave it exhausted,
With struggles for rest.

Losing it's identity by becoming everyone,
If it were somebody, then it'd be less of a person,
Fighting it's own wars and losing it's might,
If it were a person, it wouldn't stand a night.

Devoted to Nothing

I gave you the pieces,
Of my fragile heart,
But you— you wanted,
Every single part;

What is this kind of trade?
That I hurt and bleed,
Where my pain is your want,
And my scars are your need;

Parts of my flesh,
For you I sold,
Yet you called me selfish,
For keeping my bones.

The World is a Murderer

The world killed me, I say,
But somewhere
It's all my fault to expect;
The world killed me, I say,
But somewhere
I struggle to accept.

Can you unspeak the words that burnt me to ashes?
Before I even thought to die,
Now I'm just drifting away with the wind,
Because I know my death won't find me alive.

I mean who loves a girl with scars?
Especially when they're etched upon her heart?

The world killed me, I say,
I didn't deserve to be treated this way
The world killed me, I say,
All I ever wanted was someone to stay.

The world wouldn't kill me,
I granted it the power myself,
I let their words dictate my feelings
How badly can I find death?

There are a lot of things
That I don't know how to convey,
This world is my murderer
And it's immensely hard to face.

The End

This evocative poetry collection delves into the darkest corners of the human experience, laying bare the wounds of emotional self-destruction, the weight of secrets, and the struggle for hope.

Through raw, unflinching language, these poems confront the painful realities of heartache, regret, and the search for redemption. The final section, 'The Sane Blood Bath,' is a visceral, unapologetic exploration of the human condition, where tenderness and brutality entwine.

This collection is not just a reflection of my inner world but also an invitation to readers to confront their own vulnerabilities. May these poems be a testament to the resilience of the human spirit and a reminder that even in darkness, hope can be found.

Dear readers,

As I come to the end of this literary journey, I am filled with immense gratitude for each and every one of you. I'm grateful for your willingness to immerse yourselves in the world I've created.

Your support, encouragement, and enthusiasm are what make the long hours, hard work, and sacrifices worthwhile. Knowing that my words have resonated with you, has inspired you, or has simply provided a moment's escape, is the greatest reward I could ask for.

Thank you for being part of this journey. Thank you for believing in me. I am honoured, humbled, and grateful for your presence in my literary life.

With heartfelt appreciation,
Simran Dev.

www.ingramcontent.com/pod-product-compliance
Lightning Source LLC
LaVergne TN
LVHW041633070526
838199LV00052B/3340